The
HIJAB
Boutique

Michelle Khan

THE ISLAMIC FOUNDATION

Copyright © The Islamic Foundation, 2011/1432 H
Text Copyright © Michelle Khan 2011
ISBN: 978-0-86037-468-8

The Hijab Boutique
Author Michelle Khan
Editor Fatima D'Oyen
Illustrators Eman Salem
Cover/Book design & typesetting Nasir Cadir
Coordinator Anwar Cara

Published by
THE ISLAMIC FOUNDATION
Markfield Conference Centre, Ratby Lane, Markfield
Leicestershire, LE67 9SY, United Kingdom
E-mail: publications@islamic-foundation.com
Website: www.islamic-foundation.com

Quran House, P.O. Box 30611, Nairobi, Kenya

P.M.B. 3193, Kano, Nigeria

Distributed by
Kube Publishing Ltd.
Tel: +44(01530) 249230, Fax: +44(01530) 249656
E-mail: info@kubepublishing.com
Website: www.kubepublishing.com

A Cataloguing-in-Publication Data record for this book is available from the British Library

ISBN: 978-0-86037-468-8

Printed by: Imak Ofset - Turkey

CONTENTS

DEDICATION

FOR TAUFIQ IQBAL SUFI,
WHO ONCE TOLD ME
I COULD BECOME A WRITER.
NOW I AM.

THANK YOU.

1

⌒⌒⌒

MISS PEABODY'S ACADEMY AND THE IMPOSSIBLE SCHOOL ASSIGNMENT

"Listen up! Listen up! Listen up EVERYONE!"
Our classroom lights are switched off. And, back on again.

Ms. Grant sure knows how to get the attention of her students. She must've passed teacher's college with full marks. I sit up in my seat despite my itchy uniform. I am seriously plagued by Monday midday blues.

"This Thursday is International Women's Day," Ms. Grant announces with her hands on her itty-bitty hips. Her pleated, knee-length skirt stands firm. "People from around the world will be celebrating what it means to be a woman. I'd like you to bring in something that symbolizes your mother. You're all expected to present one item over the course of three class periods."

Right then, the school bell rings. Relief bursts through me. It's the end of the day! I've been operating on 'half-battery' because I stayed up late studying for this morning's math test. Everyone in my classroom is chatting away at full speed. Even Ms. Grant knows that getting anyone's attention now is a lost cause. She walks back to her desk where everything is placed 'just so'. It's clear that she has an allergy to anything messy. I wouldn't be surprised if she arranges her wardrobe according to colour at home, in alphabetical order! But my fellow students rush out of our classroom like they've got springs on their feet. I follow the crowd and get going too.

"Have a nice evening, Farah," my social studies teacher says.

"Thank you, Ms. Grant," I say, heading out the door. "The same to you."

∞ ∞

I board our school bus (a.k.a. the Banana Boat) with my best friend, Ashanti Smith. We've been BFFs (best friends forever) ever since we were toddlers. No joke. Mom says we hit it off in a baby playgroup. I guess we had an instant *connection*— before we could spell the word. We're both 'only children', and refer to ourselves as 'soul sisters'. We love to do EVERYTHING together. Naturally, we're glued to each other on the Banana Boat, too. I always get the window seat, no questions asked. In solid friendships, some things − thankfully! − are just a given.

It's no coincidence that Ashanti and I attend the same prestigious, all-girls private school. Here's the scoop: two years ago, we left our local elementary school. We set our sights on our new school after reading about it in the children's section of our local newspaper. The article explained how Miss Peabody's Academy is known state-wide for its fantastic art programmes. Why wouldn't we want to go to an environment where our talents would bloom? After all, Ashanti and I are art fanatics. We've taken Saturday morning art classes together forever. Once we found the school of our dreams, we made a case to our mothers, explaining why we wanted to attend. We must have rehearsed a million times behind closed doors in anticipation of their questions! *Alhamdulillah*, our hard work paid off. Both mothers gave us the bright green light! However, our battle was yet to be won. Next, came the admission process. F.Y.I.: places at Miss Peabody's Academy don't just depend on parents being able to afford hefty tuition fees. Prospective students have to go through a tough interview process. The teachers grilled us with questions. We answered honestly. Both Ashanti and I brought in portfolios of our artwork. And then, the day we were waiting for arrived, and — tah — dah! — the postman delivered letters welcoming us to join Miss Peabody's Academy. I can still taste the sweet double fudge sundaes we had to celebrate our combined success. Talk about yum!

Our efforts were worth it; it's a good school, with a great art programme. But Miss Peabody's Academy isn't perfect. For one thing, I'm embarrassed to admit that our school prides itself over its dinky bus rides. I personally don't see what the big deal is. The seats are comfy. Most rides are relatively short. Ben (our bus driver) always has his eyes on the road — though I'll tell you in the strictest confidence that I've caught him sneaking sips from his coffee cup whenever we stop at a red light. Anyway, this Banana Boat was a stormy subject when the idea was first introduced. Loads of parents objected to it. They wanted to keep sending out taxi cabs or chauffeurs to pick up their little princesses. Meetings were held; tempers flared. Some local Los Angeles television stations picked up the story. In the end, our school's tough board of governors won, and my mom couldn't have been happier. She said the school bus ride would make the girls at Miss Peabody's Academy more humble. To be honest, I'm not so sure.

For the record, there is no assigned seating on the Banana Boat, yet everyone always sits in the same area. Read: it's an unspoken code. Miss Peabody's has pupils ranging from little kindergarteners to mature fifth graders. You can see this divide on the bus. The youngest kids sit up front. The middle graders are smack centre. The eldest students head towards the back. However, the most prized seats in the last row of the Banana Boat are for the super-popular girls from my fifth grade class: Stacy, Tammi and Juliet. (F.Y.I.: I secretly refer to this threesome as the 'Cool as Ice' girls.)

Ashanti and I get to sit in the second-to-last row thanks to Ashanti's mom. Now, I don't want to give you the wrong idea. Ms. Smith didn't bribe anyone to get her daughter (Ashanti) and her best friend (me) better seating. Okay, okay, I admit that we did, in fact, score these seats because of Ms. Smith's celebrity status. You see, Ashanti's mom is an actress on the hit daytime TV soap opera, 'Blinding Light'. One time last year, Ashanti and I got to meet the e-n-t-i-r-e cast from her swanky show. It wasn't exactly a joyful experience, though. First, my mom went on and on about how soap operas are a waste of time. Second, the biggest actress on 'Blinding Light' wore so much perfume that I went into a sneezing frenzy. I'm not even exaggerating when I say I had a dripping, runny nose and everything. Talk about embarrassing with a capital E!

On today's bus ride home, the hot topic is the assignment about International Women's Day. I choose to look out at our sunny Los Angeles streets and stare at the incredible blue skies. I decide to listen rather than participate in the conversation. It's not that I'm being nosy; it's actually hard *not* to overhear the 'Cool as Ice' girls. Their voices are always cranked up at full volume.

"This homework assignment is totally fantastic!" Tammi, the 'Cool as Ice' girls' spokesperson announces. She flicks her fluffy, shoulder-length blonde hair. "It's hard to pick just one thing that represents my mom. She has the most amazing stuff."

I wish I had that problem, I think to myself. *My religious mother only has simple belongings.*

Juliet pops fruit-scented, sugary bubblegum behind the seat, so that the bus driver won't see her. "I know what I'm bringing in," she adds with a sparkling white smile that would surprise any dentist. "My mom is a talented makeup artist. She lives for French-label cosmetics."

Stacy crosses her long legs that seem to start at her waist. "You'll never catch my mom without a paintbrush," she says, with a hint of pride showing in her exotic eyes. "Mom loves creating artwork featuring old Chinese women."

Tammi smacks the bus seat in front of her. I start and nearly jump at her sudden, unexpected movement.

"Now I know exactly what to bring in!" Tammi exclaims with wide, turquoise eyes.

You can tell a light bulb has just gone on in her brain.

Juliet and Stacy sit at the edge of their seats. "What?" they ask, like eager beavers.

"My mom is always moving to music," Tammi singsongs. For added emphasis, she drums a beat with her palms on her lap. "Mom has the most gorgeous tap-dancing shoes. I can't wait to show them off to everyone!"

I'm not surprised that her mother is a performer, and tell Ashanti so. My best friend has a talent for spotting theatrical genes, although Ashanti didn't inherit many from her mother herself. Our whispered conversation catches the attention of the leader of the 'Cool as Ice' girls.

"Hey, Ashanti!" Tammi says, poking my BFF on her shoulder with her sharp, fiery-red nails.

Ashanti turns around to face her. "Yeah?"

Tammi crosses her arms. "I want you to bring in a script from the Blinding Light show," she orders, arching her overly-plucked eyebrow in challenge.

I can tell Ashanti is trying to hide a cringe. More often than not, she doesn't like the awkward situations she gets into because of her mom's very public job.

Stacy nods her pin-straight, midnight-black mane. "Yeah, my grandma would love to know what's going to happen next on her favourite soap opera. She taught herself English just so she could keep up with the show."

Ashanti purses her shapely, thick lips. "I know for a fact that the writers on the 'Blinding Light' keep the show's storyline top secret," she says with authority.

Nobody argues with this. It would be silly to. Everyone knows that Ashanti has a lot of insider info about the world of television.

"Getting my hands on a script definitely won't happen," Ashanti continues. "But I can do the next best thing, and bring in autographed pictures of all the actors."

Now I turn to see the reactions of the 'Cool as Ice' girls. My eyes dart from Juliet, to Tammi, to Stacy's face. Just as I predicted, they are melting with excitement. I'm happy for my best friend's triumph, but secretly I wish my classmates would react the same way to something I could bring in about MY *hijab*-wearing mother.

Ashanti meets my eyes. I can tell she's trying to read my thoughts. "You've been awfully quiet, Farah. What are you planning to bring in for International Women's Day?"

How do I tell her that we may be "soul sisters," but I'm the one whose mom is not from Hollywood? She wouldn't understand.

Her mom has been a celebrity ever since she was a child. I look out the bus window, and thankfully my stop has arrived. I throw my heavy backpack over my shoulder and get up.

"I'm still trying to chew up an idea about my mother," I tell Ashanti. I squeeze past her muscular legs and into the bus aisle. "See you tomorrow."

I get off my bus in record time. I watch the Banana Boat drive away, and feel envious because both the bus and the girls inside it know where they are heading. I start to walk up my winding, red-bricked driveway at a snail's pace. The weight of my backpack seems to test the strength of my every bone. It's almost like everything around me is drooping. The sun beats down on me. When I reach the iron gate barricading our home, it's hot and rough to touch. It silently begs to be repainted. The weeds in our front lawn dance wildly in the wind. I drag my feet to our front door, and laugh dryly at the lion statues that greet me with empty eyes. They, too, look defeated. I can't help but think they miss the absence of my doting, late father (may Allah have mercy on him). He was extravagant in every way—speech, clothing, work ethics, volunteer efforts and belongings. He wholeheartedly believed that his home was his castle. In turn, he spent many long hours plugging away at his super-successful textile business. He made sure that everything was topnotch. Ever since his death, there has been nobody in our small family to step up to the plate and take on that role. In a sense, Mom and I have wilted away with him.

I punch in the security code to our home and step inside to the cool interior. I hear the water running and figure Mom must be taking a bath. That suits me just fine. I kick off my trainers with relief and put them inside the closet. I'm about to leave the entrance hall when I do a double take and stare at the shoe rack that houses Mom's footwear collection. Not surprisingly, there isn't a pair of tap dancing shoes in sight. Forget that, Mom doesn't even own a pair of high heels! I pick up a set of modest leather flats, and smack their rubber soles together. No rhythmic sound. Their silence hangs like a heavy, dark cloud over my mind.

My heart is beating faster now. With a new sense of purpose, I march upstairs to my mother's bedroom. The soft beige carpet under my feet offers little comfort. Rushing over to the mahogany vanity bureau that I share with Mom, I open our drawer with more force than necessary. My fruit-flavoured lip glosses and rhinestone hair clips jump in surprise. I ignore them. I'm on a mission to find goodies that don't belong to me, but I don't discover any treasures. Instead, Mom's hard, plastic hairbrush stares back at me. By its side, I see a plain white hairdryer. Pricy makeup is nowhere to be seen. Once again, modesty reigns supreme.

Annoyed, I go downstairs to our living room. I want to see something—ANYTHING—that looks like the belongings of my friends' mothers'. My eyes refocus as this room refreshes me with colour. Our walls are painted a light yellow hue that matches the sunshine pouring in our large windows. Exotic plants line the floor, showing off their natural beauty. Dad's antique wooden coffee table stands proud, despite its obvious chips. His favourite cream-coloured sofa set looks plush, but at the same time it murmurs sadness over seeing better days. My eyes wander to the one-of-a-kind quilt hanging that my mom made, with its rich, Indian *sari* fabrics. I walk over and finger the quilt's delicate gold and red threads. Without needing to ask, I know this rare, handmade piece of work is too fragile to leave the safety of this room. Once again, I am defeated.

With a heavy heart, I enter our spacious kitchen. The black and white tiles underfoot feel cool under my bare feet. There aren't any snazzy portraits of people or funky posters in this section of our house either. From across the room, I see stained glass artwork that Ashanti and I made together. Its cheerful colours mock me. Why does this school assignment have to be so difficult? Is it really so hard for my family to be like everyone else's?

I sit down on a bar stool at our marble kitchen island. Its gleaming countertop is as shiny as the wet tears that threaten to pour out of my eyes. I blink them away. As usual, Mom has already prepared an after-school snack for me. My stomach grumbles just looking at the plate. I pick up my *halal* roast beef sandwich loaded with delicious toppings, say a quiet *'bismillah'* and take a bigger bite than usual. I swallow hard, trying to gulp down my problems with good food. My eyes are drawn to a note left for me on the counter. I know it's from Mom because it's written on her pale pink stationery. She has a quirky but lovable habit of leaving me surprise letters. I pick up today's message in slow motion.

As-Salamu Alaykum Farah,
Hope you had a wonderful day at school, honey.
I know you had a math test earlier this morning, and inshallah you did very well. I thought I'd treat you to your favourite sandwich for all your hard work.
Enjoy your food, and get some rest while I have a relaxing bath. You can start on your homework after you feel fresh.
Love you,
Mom xo

I usually grin after reading one of Mom's surprise notes. Right now, I can't even force a fake smile. I'm just too upset about not being like everyone else! Don't get me wrong. I know there are A LOT of kids out there who'd trade their favourite video game collection in a heartbeat to have a mom like mine. Translation: In this sense, I am grateful for my wonderful, loving mother. However, having a great mom is what makes this situation all the more complicated. Before this, I could always run to her if anything went topsy-turvy. I can't do that now without hurting Mom's feelings. After all, there's no polite way to tell someone that all her belongings are b-o-r-i-n-g. What am I supposed to do???

I decide to take my mind off my problems for a little while, and do my afternoon prayers. Maybe Allah will give me an inspiration. I splash cool water over my face, arms, head and feet, taking special care around my ears. Making ablutions always makes me feel fresh and tingly after the hot and dusty ride home. But although the peace that comes with prayer calms down my nerves, after my final *salam* my heart is still troubled. There's no solution yet in sight. Conclusion: I'm still stuck!

2

⤜⤛⤚

ME, THE INVISIBLE GIRL?

The next week zips by. International Women's Day has come and gone. We're currently on the third and final day of presentations, and my sense of dread starts to build up. I managed to avoid being called on both last Thursday and Friday. Forget having the Monday blues today – I've got a serious case of nervous butterflies. Once again, I've come to school empty-handed. Guilt over skipping a homework assignment sits in my belly like a heavy rock. This is definitely a new and super-uncomfortable experience for me.

The last presentation is concluding. My classmate, Roxanne, is passing around different fancy-schmancy anklets that her mother's company makes.

"Please handle these items with care, girls!" Ms. Grant says. "Most of these anklets are made with real gems cast in gold and silver."

"Yes, my momma gave me this stuff on loan," Roxanne says so quietly in her Texan accent that you practically have to fall out of your seat to hear her.

The prized anklets that are circulating land in Tammi's hands. She naturally has to make a splash as the leader of the 'Cool as Ice' girls. In a blink of an eye, Tammi rolls up the hem of her uniform and tries on a pair of anklets.

"How do I look?" Tammi asks, standing up and strutting her stuff like a model on an imaginary catwalk.

I half expect my fellow classmates to break out in applause. While this doesn't happen, our room is abuzz with excitement.

"She looks absolutely stunning," I hear girls whisper from the desks behind me.

Tammi has gone from popular student to celebrity extraordinaire.

"Jeez, those anklets make some noise!" Juliet, another of the 'Cool as Ice' girls says.

'Who would've thought that Roxanne's got a momma who makes tinkling, jingling anklets?' I say to myself. After all, Roxanne is THE quietest student in our class. If you ask me, that's pretty *ironic*. Boy, would my English teacher be proud that I just used one of her spelling test words. I know for a fact that my mom would never wear a pair of noisy anklets. Not because anklets are a 'fashion don't' or anything. Rather, our holy book, the *Qur'an*, states that women shouldn't wear anything that makes noise when they walk. Yes, my mom is different yet again.

Once the last of the anklets has finished circulating, I sink deep into my seat, hoping against hope that Ms. Grant won't notice me. I wish I could press a secret button under my desk to become the Invisible Girl. Why haven't scientists come up with this invention? Why, why, why? *'Oh Allah, please, please, please don't let her call on me,'* I silently pray.

It's too late. Ms. Grant looks at me directly. "You're up next, Farah Khan. In fact, you're the last student remaining to present."

It turns out Allah has another plan for me. Perspiration trickles down my back.

Suddenly, an age-old excuse pops into my head. "Um, Ms. Grant," I blurt out nervously, "I don't actually have anything to present. My, er, dog ate my homework."

My classmates hoot with laughter.

"Nice one, Farah!" someone cheers.

I'm not in the mood to be congratulated. I didn't mean to be funny, and deep in my heart I know I shouldn't have lied about it, not even a white lie like this one. But my lame excuse came blurting out on account of desperation. Feeling totally ill at ease, I sink even deeper into my seat. If only the floor would swallow me whole!

"That's enough," Ms. Grant says firmly, cutting into my thoughts and into the chuckles rippling through the room. "Farah, I'd like to speak to you privately. Everyone else is dismissed, as there are no further presentations."

As expected, there are no objections to an early exit. Girls practically fly out of our classroom. As I approach my teacher it feels like lead weights are strapped to my feet.

Ms. Grant takes a seat behind her desk. "Would you care to tell me what's going on?"

I stand before her like a soldier who's been caught deserting his post. Words struggle to escape my dry tongue.

Ms. Grant isn't rattled by my silence. "I know you don't have a pet pooch, Farah. I remember the excellent paper you wrote on 'Islam and Animals'."

Guilt splatters cherry-coloured paint across my cheeks. I don't know what I was thinking when I told that lie. "You're right, Ms. Grant," I state quietly, with my shoes shuffling. "We don't have any dogs."

"Frankly, I don't know what to make of this," Ms. Grant admits, fingering a manilla file folder on her desk. "You usually put two hundred percent effort into your assignments."

I nod in agreement.

"I don't mean to pry," Ms. Grant says delicately, "but is everything okay at home?"

"Yes!" I cry abruptly. "I mean, everything is great at home."

"Then what is it?"

I decide to be honest. There's no point in denying my dilemma any longer. My head hangs so low that my dark hair masks my vision. "The truth is... my mother...is, well... boring."

"Oh, my word!" Ms. Grant states, throwing her liver-spotted hand to her chest. "I can't believe you said that. I've met Mrs. Khan at parent-teacher conferences and she's not dull in the least."

I shake my head fiercely. "She's not like the other girls' moms!" I yelp. "I searched my house from top to bottom looking for something interesting to present, but I came up with nothing."

Ms. Grant crosses her arms squarely. "I find that hard to believe. I'm giving you one more week to find something. Otherwise, you'll be subject to detention, young lady."

I swallow a gulp the size of a football. I've never been in any teacher's bad books before.

∞∞

I find Ashanti waiting for me outside our classroom. I'm so happy to see my loyal friend that I give her a great bear hug. I tell Ashanti about my one-week deadline. I'm in serious panic mode because I have no idea how I'll find anything. We walk to the Banana Boat together, trying to think up a solution.

Ashanti scrunches up her forehead in deep thought. "Why don't you tell everyone about your mom's knack for art?" she suggests.

"No, that won't do," I say, shrugging off her idea.

Okay, it's true. My mom makes a killer paper mache paste, and she made the beautiful quilt hanging in our living room. But she isn't exactly the next Pablo Picasso.

"I don't see why you can't talk about your mom's artistic talents," Ashanti persists. "She's held craft parties for us every Monday night since we were four years old."

I still won't budge. "The last thing I want is for everyone to think of us as toddlers who still like to cut and paste – not in our school!"

"You're such a stubborn mule!" Ashanti laughs, putting her strong arm around my shoulder. "But I get your point. I _am_ looking forward to what your mom has planned for us this evening, though."

3

⌘

MY MOTHER'S SECRET LIFE

Unfortunately, things at home are not what I expected. Not in a good way either. You'd think a tornado just whipped through the house! My mother's prized spotless kitchen is upside down. Boxes are everywhere. Mom is buried behind a stack of old photos. Not only that, she's distracted when Ashanti and I enter.

"As-salamu 'alaykum, Mom," I say, clearing my throat loudly to get her attention.

My mother's bright green eyes open in surprise. "Wa 'alaykum as-salam, honey. I didn't even hear you two come in." She smiles at Ashanti. "How's Farah's favourite 'soul sister' keeping?"

"Couldn't be better, Mrs. Khan!" Ashanti says, sticking her two thumbs up.

My eyes dart about, trying to figure out what we'll be doing this evening. "Mom, are we going to make some kind of photo collage?"

My mother gives a little laugh and fiddles with her shoulder-length, straight black hair. This is a sure sign that something's on her mind.

"Um, no, honey," Mom says apologetically. "I actually forgot all about our arts and crafts night!" She glances at the pictures in front of her. "I'm sorry; I guess I got carried away."

I feel my temper rise. After the rough day I've had at school, I was really looking forward to relaxing with a fun project. "How unfair, Mom!" I complain, dropping my backpack on the ground.

As usual, good old Ashanti tries to keep the peace. "Don't worry about it, Mrs. Khan," she says, with a quick wave of her hand. "You've got a PERFECT track record. This is the first time you've forgotten in, like, seven years. Sometimes I wonder if my mom even remembers my middle name."

"Don't say that," Mom replies, getting up from our kitchen table. She cups Ashanti's face affectionately. "I know for a fact that your mother loves you very much."

Mom squeezes both of our shoulders. "You children are the most precious gift from Allah—or God, as our Christian friends say. Don't ever, ever forget that."

I feel myself soften. "Moms are pretty special, too." I kiss the side of my mother's lightly-tanned cheek, feeling like a dork for my earlier actions.

"Okay, ladies, cut out all the mushy stuff!" Ashanti interrupts.

Mom pinches Ashanti's young cheek. "We love you, too, silly girl."

We all laugh together.

My eyes wander back to the scattered photographs laying everywhere. "So, what's the deal with all these pictures?"

Mom leads us to the kitchen table. "I was walking down memory lane," she says. Her beautiful eyes remain distant. "I was trying to figure out my life journey. I wanted to remember and reflect on how I got to where I am today."

Mom motions for us to sit down, and picks up a set of pictures to explain. The first photo catches me off guard. It's a family portrait. My eyes are glued to the image of my late father. His winning smile pierces my heart. I don't talk much about my dad—not even with Ashanti. It's been more than two years since he died, but it still hurts too much.

"As you know, Mr. Khan's death was very sudden," Mom says to Ashanti. "He went out to fetch some milk at night, and a drunk driver hit him. In a split second his life was over…" Mom says softly, caressing the family portrait in her hand. "May Allah have mercy on him. My biggest regret is that I never had a chance to say goodbye."

A wild tide of emotions hits my stomach. "I miss him so much, Mom," I blurt aloud.

Mom brushes my coffee-coloured hair with her fingertips. "So do I, honey. *Inshallah* we will all be together in Paradise one day."

Ashanti peers closer at the photograph. "You look gorgeous, Mrs. Khan! I mean, you're still very pretty, but I've forgotten how much you really decked yourself out back then. Your makeup and jewellery were so funky."

Mom bites her lip in thought. "I don't feel like dressing up anymore," she says. "I used to enjoy beautifying myself for my husband. Now that I'm a widow, I have no desire to wear lipstick or other makeup at home."

This is the first time Mom has admitted this in my presence. However, now that I think about it, her appearance has changed since Dad passed away. She practically never wears her long, flowing dresses. She's always running errands in tired-looking jeans, and a long top. Ever so slowly, small lines have crept into her face. I always thought her plain appearance had to do with her hectic schedule—not because she just wanted to look pretty for Dad. How did I not connect the dots?

Mom lightens the mood, pulling out some old photographs she found of Ashanti and me. There is one of a trip the three of us made to the Los Angeles Zoo and Botanical Gardens. Then, there's a picture of an arts and crafts night from long ago—we were finger painting puppets made out of paper bags. Ashanti had serious style even at five years old. She's gone through more hairdos than a baby goes through diapers! Her hair is constantly updated with different styles courtesy of Ms. Smith's 'Blinding Light' personal hairstylist.

The last picture we see is of Mom making a speech to her graduating class at UCLA (for those of you who aren't from sunny California, that's the University of California, Los Angeles).

"I had the honour of speaking there because I was named valedictorian of my class," Mom tells us. She looks fondly at the photograph of her standing at a podium in a cap and gown. "Valedictorian means top student. I worked very hard, and earned good grades in my business program."

Ashanti shakes her head. "I don't get it, Mrs. Khan," she says, wondering. "Why didn't you make a great career for yourself as a businesswoman with your awesome grades?"

Mom smiles. "I actually was a career woman when I first got married," she tells us. "In fact, I worked as a financial advisor for a Fortune 500 company. I left my job when Farah was born."

This is news to me. Mom doesn't usually talk much about her past. This admission of hers has got me curious, and at this point it doesn't add up. "I don't see why you'd have to quit your job after having me," I say.

Mom entwines her long fingers together. "It was a personal choice," she explains. "I stopped working because your Dad made enough money to support us without an added paycheck from me." Mom looks at me thoughtfully. "I felt it was more important that I devote myself to your needs than to build a career for myself. Work was a great challenge, and fun, but it also required a lot of long hours away from home. I didn't want to come home exhausted every night, too tired to give you and your father enough love and attention. So I became a stay-at-home-Mom," she remarks with a smile.

"Wow!" Ashanti exclaims with a gasp. "That's really sweet, Mrs. Khan. That's a big sacrifice."

"I don't want to give you girls the wrong idea," Mom says to us quickly. "Every woman's life story and choices are unique." She looks at Ashanti directly now. "Society isn't always kind to single, working women. Your mom has done exceptionally well despite everything she's faced. You should be proud of her."

Just as Mom says this, Ashanti's stomach and mine growl in unison—proof that we're 'soul sisters.'

"You poor kids!" Mom says, getting up immediately. "We've been so busy talking that I haven't even fed you anything. You must be so hungry after a long day at school!"

Mom takes off to grind up some meat at lightning speed.

Ashanti pats her empty belly. "I may have a housekeeper with a fancy cooking school degree, but I love your mom's home-cooked food," she says, licking her lips. "Mrs. Khan makes awesome *shish kebabs*. You're one lucky girl!"

Ashanti gets her wish. Mom does end up making *shish kebabs* for dinner, and Ashanti goes home like a happy camper.

∽◌∾

Late in the evening I go to Mom's bedroom closet to snoop through her stuff. I have exactly one week to find something to present at school. The countdown has begun. I've heard awful things about what happens to kids in detention. Teachers make you wash chalkboards with rags that previous students in detention have spat on. Read: Yuck, yuck and yuck. I need to find something fast. It doesn't help that I'm standing on a wobbly stool. If I could just reach the top shelf! I see a big, inviting box up there marked "Sisters Parties." Maybe my mother has some cool frocks and cosmetics tucked inside. Muslim women have the freedom to dress up to the max at these social events. I've seen Mom and her best friend, Aunty Sheila, wear some drool-worthy outfits to Muslim Sister Parties. But my mother's daily wear is more simple. The only things I've found in the room so far are long-sleeved cotton shirts, a few faded *shalwar kameez* and other traditional Indian clothes. At last, my fingers grasp my target. Trying to balance, I pull the box down, legs and fingers shaking. My conscience tells me I should be respecting my mom's privacy, but I just don't know what else to do.

"What are you looking for, Farah?"

I'm caught totally off guard. I fall off the wobbly stool and land flat on my face. Talk about busted! I feel like a criminal who's been caught red-handed.

Mom puts out her soft hand. "Are you alright, honey?"

I latch on and get up. "I'm okay," I say, brushing off my clothes. "I'm sorry, Mom," I mumble, staring at the floor.

My brain goes into a tizzy now, telling my heart to confess to Mom about what's really going on. *How can I do that???* I wonder to myself. The last thing I want to do is to hurt my mother's feelings. Read: I just have to find a solution by myself.

"I, er, wasn't looking for, um, anything in particular," I blurt out another white lie. "Just, you know, browsing."

Mom's fingers toy with one of her long strands of hair, like she does when something is up. I'm caught off guard once again. "Have you figured out what I've been up to?" she asks sheepishly.

I look at her, genuinely confused. "What do you mean?"

Mom stares at the beige carpet under our feet. "I'm sorry for keeping this 'arrangement' from you," she says with remorse. "I know we share everything, and it must hurt knowing that I've kept you in the dark. I just wanted everything to be finalized before I got you involved. I hope you can understand."

My stomach flip-flops. "What do you mean—what's going on?" I ask, a million bad scenarios zooming through my mind.

Mom gently takes my hand. "There's nothing to worry about, Farah," she reassures me. "Let me just start at the beginning."

I nod.

Mom crinkles the corners of her large eyes. "First, I'll test your knowledge about why I started wearing *hijab*," she says playfully, raising a naturally arched eyebrow. "Tell me: why do you think I made the choice to become a *hijabi*?"

"Simple!" I answer, thoroughly enjoying our game. "You wear a *hijab* because your beauty is so special, it's private. You only want to share it with the people you're closest to—like your child, husband, parents, brothers and sisters."

"You're on the right track," Mom responds with a smile. "However, your answer applies to most Muslim *hijabi* women. I want you to think of why exactly *your* mother started to wear *hijab*."

I stand in front of Mom like a bump on a log. I'm stumped. The truth is, I never thought much about why she made this change in lifestyle and appearance. "You've got me, Mom," I admit, waving my hands in surrender. "I guess I don't know the real reason why *you're* a *hijabi*."

"Well, now I'll tell you," Mom answers candidly, her voice taking on a more serious tone. "As you know, I didn't know much about Islam until I was an adult. My family never practiced much; they just went to Eid prayers and special occasions like weddings or funerals. I only began taking religious classes after I got married."

I nod in recognition of her past and present. "Yeah, I know how much you look forward to the weekend study circles for women at our mosque."

"Well, it was during one of those classes," Mom goes onto say, "that I learned that the Prophet Muhammad, peace and blessings be upon him, taught us that girls should start wearing *hijab* once they reach puberty, and that the Holy Qur'an says Muslim women should wear loose clothing and cover everything except our hands and face. The women there had a long and animated discussion about it. Some of them, like me, had wrongly believed that covering up was just an Arab custom, or cultural practice." Mom runs her slender fingers through her hair. "To make a long story short, I couldn't get those verses out of my mind. It felt as if Allah was speaking directly to me."

"So what'd you do about it?" I ask, curious.

Mom's emerald eyes float past me. "I read every book and every opinion out there about *hijabs*. I spoke to our *Imam*. I poured my heart out in prayer. Finally, I knew that I had to take that step." Mom pauses, and raises her head. "I became the first woman in my family to become a *hijabi*. At least, the first woman in living memory. My great-grandmothers must have also worn *hijab,* and the generations before them."

I don't know a lot about my mother's family. The gist of what I know is that my grandmother died of cancer when I was a baby, and other relatives died in a cholera epidemic in India years ago. I don't want to bring this up now, so I change the topic. I recall the change Mom made in how she dressed. "I was about seven years old when you first started to wear *hijab*," I say.

"That's right," Mom says, confirming my memory. "Your dad was with us back then, too."

My stomach automatically turns at the mention of my late father. "What did Dad have to say about your decision?"

"He was away on business when I made my intention to wear *hijab*," Mom recalls with her face brightening at the memory. "I actually surprised him at the airport when I went to pick him up. I just showed up in a headscarf!"

My eyes open wide. "How did he react?"

"Well, your dad wasn't enthusiastic in the beginning," Mom answers honestly. "He was afraid for me—afraid that I'd be discriminated against." She takes a deep breath. "Non-Muslims interpret *hijab* in different ways. Some think that it has to do with politics; others believe that it is a sign of women being oppressed. Some people feel that it is the duty of foreigners to fit in, or they may even feel a bit threatened by *hijab*. They haven't read the Qur'an or teachings of our beloved Prophet (peace be upon him) and simply don't understand. Or they may not understand the importance of religious freedom, and its long tradition in this country. Your dad didn't want me to experience any more racism or Islamophobia than necessary. He was trying to protect me."

"So how did you convince Dad?" I ask, curiously. My father had always seemed so supportive.

"I didn't back down," Mom replies with a grin. "Your dad saw how important *hijab* is to me, and he accepted my choice. And after I showed him the Qur'anic verses and hadiths of the Prophet (peace be upon him), he also realized that our dress code is part of Allah's guidance and the way of Islam. Yes, it's true that strangers sometimes give me curious or even angry stares. However, when people ask questions I use the opportunity to spread the word and message of Islam."

My head is spinning with all this info. "I feel so stupid, Mom," I admit as I plop onto the floor of her walk-in closet, "not knowing any of these things about you."

Mom shakes her head. "That's perfectly normal," she says, adding, "You were still a young child. I waited to share this with you until you were mature enough to understand my choices. Now you are growing up. You'll be a young woman soon enough yourself."

I am only half-listening now, and my mind wanders to what led us into this conversation in the first place. "You still haven't explained the 'arrangement' you've been keeping from me!"

Mom looks at me, surprised. "You really don't know what I've been up to?"

I shake my head quickly. "No, I don't."

"In that case, I'll take you to the place that's about to change our life," Mom says with great purpose. "Everything will make more sense then. *Bismillah* – let's go!"

She takes my hand and we hurry downstairs, two steps at a time.

4

❧

DREAMS, AMBITIONS AND THE HIJAB BOUTIQUE

Mom grabs the keys to Dad's gold convertible. I try to play cool, but my emotions are getting the better of me. I begin to sweat. What she's about to tell me is big – I can feel it in my stomach. It's also totally logical because, until today, we've NEVER taken Dad's beloved car out for a spin. Why, you ask? Simple. It's because our memories of him are so deeply connected to this vehicle. He bought it after scoring a huge business contract. At the time, both Mom and I knew n-o-t-h-i-n-g about his big purchase. One afternoon, Dad surprised us by zooming into our driveway in a shiny convertible. The rooftop of his brand new car was down, and he shouted gleefully to Mom and I that our lives were about to change. He was right: we watched the only man in our lives be transformed from an ordinary businessman into Mr. Textile Mogul, and our lives were transformed right along with him. My heart still bursts with pride over his achievements.

F.Y.I.: Dad's success didn't just benefit us; he also improved the lives of poor people. He donated heavily to homeless shelters in particular. Like I said earlier, Dad believed that a man's home is his castle. He felt that this should apply to temporary housing, too. He worked very hard to make the homeless shelters in our area become beautiful, safe havens. Dad felt this was his duty as a fortunate Muslim, because he knew that his business would never have taken off if it had not been Allah's will. He used to tell me, "Remember, Farah, that it is the poor people's right to receive *zakat* and charity: our wealth can only be purified by sharing it with others.' His heart was truly made of gold. It's only fitting that his favourite car was the same colour.

My mind's eye is flooded with memories, and my body finds it difficult to keep up with its emotionally-fuelled images. I feel like I can't breathe. Mom and I have long stopped chattering. We exit our home in silence, only stopping when we reach the entrance to our three-door garage. Mom punches in the security code, and just as programmed, the doors rise up slowly to let us in. Under normal circumstances this action is routine for me, but today everything is different. I allow my eyes to glance at the side of our garage where my dad's convertible is parked. For the first time in the two years since his death, I find the courage to stare at the symbolic fruit of his hard work. A ray of Los Angeles sunshine hits the gold coat and temporarily blinds my vision. I squint, and turn to face Mom.

"Are you ready?" Mom asks, her tender green eyes searching mine. "I arranged for the car to have a complete tune-up yesterday; it's all set to go."

Feeling a rush of adrenaline, my head bobs up-and-down, nodding 'yes'.

We hop into the car. Mom turns the ignition key and the convertible smoothly pulls out of the garage, engine humming.

Mom lowers the top of Dad's convertible, and the unforgiving sun beats down on us as we drive. Wisps of my dark hair fly in every direction, scattered by the wind. Mom's checkered-patterned *hijab* is tousled, too. We zip out of our neighbourhood in record time. We drive past Miss Peabody's Academy and I immediately think back on the times Dad dropped me off to school in this very car. An old wound opens up inside of me. My hands seek comfort by clinging to my leather seat, but it, too, burns with its heat. I look up at the palm trees lining the road, thankful that these old friends smile down at me. To my surprise, Mom pulls our car into a small shopping centre.

Once we park, Mom drums her fingers on the steering wheel that was once held by Dad.

"Farah...I...er..." she begins to say, but her tongue stumbles before she can complete her sentence.

"Is everything okay, Mom?" I ask, the tension mounting up inside me.

Mom quickly takes her hands off the steering wheel and places them over mine. She squeezes my hands tight. "We'll be fine, honey," she answers firmly. "We're troopers who can handle any change, so long as we're together."

I'm becoming more puzzled by the minute. "What type of 'change' are you talking about, Mom?"

Mom takes a deep breath. She looks absently at the mall in front of us. "Farah, have you noticed anything different about the appearance of our house?"

"Well..." I say, thinking long and hard, "Our house has been stuck in time since Dad passed away," I finally answer. "Our furniture is getting worn and old. Paint is peeling in the kitchen and the bathroom. And our front lawn has become a wild jungle of weeds."

"Do you know why I haven't taken care of those things?" Mom asks.

"Umm...," I respond, "You haven't been able to deal with those things because it hurts too much to take over Dad's role?"

Mom smiles at me, and gently touches my cheek. "No, honey, that's not the reason," she says softly. "I struggle to maintain the upkeep of our house because I can barely make ends meet. Our two sources of income are savings and Dad's investment money from the stock market. Stocks haven't been doing too well, and now our money is beginning to run out."

It feels like a ton of bricks have just fallen from the sky and crashed onto my head. I start to feel dizzy.

"Oh my goodness!" Mom exclaims, quickly grabbing a bottle of water from her purse. "Drink up. You look like you're going to be sick."

I accept her offer of nature's drink and take a sip, but I don't really feel better. Seeing the worry lines on my mother's delicate forehead, though, I say, "I'm okay, Mom."

"Correction," Mom says, taking me squarely by the shoulders. "We'll be okay." She looks at me with twinkling eyes. "I have a plan!"

I sit up straight. "You do?"

"Yes, inshallah." Mom says proudly. "I've figured out a way to earn an income and still care for you." She pauses to look at the numerous shops that stand before us. "I'm opening up a business in this mall with Aunty Sheila. We're calling it, 'The Hijab Boutique.'"

"Wow!" I exclaim. "That's amazing news, Mom."

Mom gives me a modest smile. "Inshallah our business, 'The Hijab Boutique,' will be a success," she says hopefully. "I intend to use the first earnings from the store to fix up our house. My plan is to sell our home, put our extra belongings up for sale and buy a smaller house to free up some cash for investment – and to live on."

"Why do we have to move?" I ask quietly, worry clawing at my heart. "I've never lived anywhere else. It feels like everything is being taken away from me." I start to think about the things I love about our house and our neighbourhood, my room full of years of art projects, our neighbours…

"Change is a part of life, Farah," Mom says, interrupting my thoughts. "Although I understand that continuity is important, too, especially for girls your age. I know how much you value Miss Peabody's Academy, and I will do my best to see that you still get to study there." She pauses to stroke my hair. "We have no choice, honey, but to move to a smaller home that we can afford. There is one thing, though, that we're taking with us for sure…"

"What's that?" I ask.

"Dad's convertible!" she laughs, throwing her hands in the air, "Your father worked hard to earn this car, and I will do my best with this business in order to keep this tangible memory of his. I can't bring myself to sell it."

I let out a sigh of relief. "That sounds good to me, Mom."

"I'm glad," Mom says with a wink. "Now, let's stop talking and let me show you my second baby, 'The Hijab Boutique!'"

The store itself is small. The whole room is occupied by scattered boxes. My eyes note the undressed mannequins and a cash register that promises to ring up sales.

"Yikes, is this place messy!" Mom states with an infectious laugh. "Would you like to help me get the shop under control?"

I smile. "I'd love to give you a hand."

Mom picks up a box lickety-split. "The main priority on today's agenda is to organize our merchandise," she declares. "Let's get started with the *hijabs*."

Together we open the seal of the first box. I see fabrics in so many colours that my eyes do a figurative cartwheel. A rainbow looks dull in comparison to these materials.

Mom notes my expression. "These *hijabs* are made of Egyptian cotton," she explains. "They come in twenty-four shades."

I recognize this *hijab* style in a jiffy. "You always wear this look to the mall," I say, feeling the cool-to-touch fabrics. "You call it your: 'no fuss, no muss appearance.' I also like to wear them for prayer.'"

"Right," Mom says with a laugh. "These *hijabs* are known as the 'one-piece.' I like them because they're quick to wear – simply slip on a tube that covers your hair, neck and shoulders, and *voila*! – you're good to go!"

We carefully place the one-piece *hijabs* on the display shelves. Then it's time to open another box once we're happy with our work. This time, I find rectangular-shaped materials with detailed embroidery. I run my hands over the fine threads that make up pictures of flowers and stars. Talk about beautiful craftsmanship!

"These *hijabs* are known as the *shayla*," Mom says. "You can wear this cut of fabric in many different styles, actually."

My brain suddenly has a flashback. "I remember you wearing a hip *shayla* head wrap style to a Muslim Sisters' Party. Aunty Sheila helped you put the look together."

"My, my, daughter," Mom says teasingly, "your memory serves you correctly. Do you think you can copy that style on a mannequin?"

"You bet!" I state, taking one rectangular piece of fabric. "I'm always up for a challenge." I skip over to a nearby mannequin and start my work. I twist and turn the *hijab* this way and that until I'm satisfied. At last I arrange it to my own satisfaction. "What do you think?" I ask nervously.

Mom comes to inspect my efforts. She turns the mannequin from side-to-side, then looks at me. "I'm impressed," she says.

I bask in the warmth of her compliment.

We now cautiously open another box, taking care not to damage any of the valuable contents. This time, I know what I'm looking at. "These are Kuwaiti *hijabs*, right?"

"You're on a definite roll today, Farah," Mom remarks. "Right again."

Curiosity gets the better of me. "Can I try on a Kuwaiti *hijab*?"

"Of course, honey," Mom says, lifting one out of a box. "Come stand in front of me so I can help you arrange it properly."

I do as I'm told. Mom starts her magic right away. She first slips a beaded tube onto my head, to go under the scarf. Then she takes a long piece of cloth, drapes it loose at one side of my head, and wraps it around the back of my head to my opposite temple, pinning it into place above my ear.

"There—we're all done," Mom says, stepping back to admire me. "*Mashallah*, you look like a Muslim princess!"

I dash off to the dressing room mirror. I turn from left to right, then spin around. "I definitely like what I'm seeing, Mom!"

We open up another box once the Kuwaiti *hijabs* are put on display. I discover pieces of square fabric in mind-boggling patterns—even in hippy-style tie dye.

"These are square *hijabs*," Mom explains. "You can be really creative in the way you wear these. You'll often see the square *hijab* photographed in editorial fashion spreads."

To emphasize her point, Mom goes behind the store's cash register and pulls out a stack of magazines, and hands them to me.

I can't believe my eyes. "I had no idea that *hijabis* had their own fashion magazines!"

Mom laughs. "We sure do. As you can see, *hijab* doesn't mean you have to look ugly. Looking modest and decent is important, but you can still look nice."

I flip through glossy page after page. "I'm impressed, Mom. These magazines are seriously neat. I always did wonder what you were reading."

Mom winks. "Now you know. Not that that's all I read, of course!"

"No, of course not," I reply, remembering the thick volumes on the history of India, classic novels and various books on Islam that fill our livingroom bookshelves.

Mom and I start to set up the Muslim fashion magazines and women's magazines that will be for sale at 'The Hijab Boutique'. Then we stand in front of our last of the small boxes. I wonder what treasures it contains. Mom opens it, and I gasp with delight. The box is filled with ribbons, dangling tassels, chiffon, silk and glittering sequins.

"These are the fancy party *hijabs* that our Muslim sisters wear at weddings, on Eid or at all-girls get-togethers," Mom explains.

I feel the glamorous materials at hand. "These *hijabs* are really beautiful…"

Mom's lips turn up in a smile. "So are you."

Together we dress up some mannequins with party *hijabs*. Finally, we stand in front of the large boxes in the corner. Mom asks me to open them, and I do. This time a selection of long denim dresses, shawls, Saudi-style *abayas*, and raincoat-type cloaks meets my eyes.

"As you know, these garments complete the Muslim outerwear look," Mom explains. "They help us protect our modesty."

Mom and I take the overgarments and put them on the different mannequins, arranging some of the *hijabs* over the coats and cloaks. In seconds, their nakedness is masked from view.

"Are we all done?" I ask once all the empty boxes have been thrown away.

"As a matter of fact, you haven't seen everything," Mom says. "Aunty Sheila and I have other things tucked away in the storage room that we'll be selling here which will help to bring in extra income." She takes my hand. "Come on, let me show you."

The storage room is cooler than the storefront. Its wooden shelves are stacked with an incredible amount of stuff, some of which I recognize.

"Let me try to guess everything that's here, okay, Mom?" I ask.

"Go for it," she says.

"Hmmm," I say, tapping my cheek with my finger. "There's kohl, incense, black seed oil, and honey." I now stand on my tiptoes to see the uppermost shelf. "Oh, and let me add prayer carpets, silver jewellery and Islamic diaries to that list." I look at Mom. "How did I do?"

Mom laughs. "You've done a great job, Miss Investigator. You spotted just about everything." She extends her arm to the top shelf. "You just left out these two items – although, in your defence, they're small and hard to see from your angle."

Mom lowers her hands and I pull them open. Sparkling pins meet my eyes, while my nostrils are met by breathtaking aromas. "What have you got there, Mom?"

Mom first shows me a pin with a pink rhinestone heart dangling from it. "This is a *hijab* pin. We can use these pins to keep our *hijabs* in place with style."

My fingers play with the pin's dangling heart. "How cool!"

Mom then opens her other palm to reveal tiny bottles marked 'pure essential oil', with names like 'sandalwood', 'amber' and 'musk'.

"These are natural perfumes, essential oils made without alcohol," Mom explains. "I'm holding three different scents in my hand. Have a sniff."

I inspect each bottle and put them close to my nose. "Wow, these perfumes smell divine!"

Mom dabs a tiny drop of amber essential oil on my neck and plants a kiss on my cheek. "These oils are very strong and Muslim women shouldn't wear them outside or in the company of strange men, but we'll be heading home soon and you're still a girl," Mom says, smiling. I smile back, enjoying the exotic scent.

☙❧

Our work finished, we tidy up the last bits of packaging and then Mom and I exit her new store space.

"Let's pick up some vanilla milkshakes after all our hard work," Mom tells me. "Then we'll have to head home. I want to be home before dark, and we need to say our evening prayers on time."

"You won't hear any objections from me!" I say, as we walk to the convertible.

Mom laughs. "That's good."

"Mom..." I say, with sudden heartfelt emotion. "I hope and pray that 'The Hijab Boutique' will be a big hit."

Mom squeezes my hand. "Thank you. *Inshallah.* "

"And I think that your *hijabs* are really special. I can't wait to show them to the girls at school, to show how they represent you."

"Is this for a school assignment?" she asks.

I nod.

Mom puts her arm around me. "Tell me more about it..."

5

❦

HIJABS IN THE SPOTLIGHT

I'm standing in front of my class.

Everyone is staring at me.

Zillions of butterflies are fluttering in my stomach.

I'm all set to give my International Women's Day presentation, and I'm just waiting for my cue to begin. I may be a few days late, but I've met Ms. Grant's deadline. This means I won't have to wash any chalkboards with dirty spat-on rags. Yay! Okay, all this nervous energy is making me slightly hyper. I must remember to breathe. 'In. Out. In. Out. Repeat. Be calm,' I say to myself.

Ms. Grant switches our classroom lights on and off. "Listen up! Listen up! Listen up, EVERYONE!" she shouts to our unruly class. "Farah is now ready to begin her presentation."

Ms. Grant looks at me and waves her hand with an imaginary flag. Translation: like a race car driver, I've been given the signal to take off. I begin by tapping into my 'honesty well'.

"This has been the toughest assignment I've ever had to do," I admit to my fellow classmates with clammy hands. "I really struggled to find something to present about my mother."

I hear Tammi release a fake cough to cover her snicker. The other 'Cool as Ice' girls, Juliet and Stacy, copy her. I totally ignore them. *Nobody and nothing will stop me today*, my inner voice tells me.

I clear my throat loudly to regain everyone's attention. "I turned my house upside down looking for something that resembles what all of you have brought in about your mothers. Only I didn't find anything like that. As a result, I thought my mother seemed pretty boring in comparison," I state. "That's why I came to school empty-handed."

Normally quiet Roxanne lets out a gasp. Even the puff of air she releases from her lips is tinged by her Texan accent.

Ashanti catches my eye. She smiles at me broadly. I take it as my cue to continue.

"This may have been the toughest assignment of my life, but it's also been the most eye-opening," I explain, with my head held high. "I've learnt a lot in the last few days about my mother. I see her under a new light now. Yes, she's 'different'—but those differences make her unique. Without them, she wouldn't be the person that I love."

"Cut to the chase, Farah," Tammi says, rolling her turquoise eyeballs. "What have you brought in to show about your mother?"

"Mind your manners, young lady," Ms. Grant cautions. "Farah's experiences are relevant to this class assignment."

Ms. Grant looks at me. "Carry on, dear."

"For today's presentation, I've brought in my mother's most obvious *outward* difference—her *hijab* collection," I announce.

Stacy throws her silky black hair behind her shoulders, and shoots up her slender hand. "I've heard the word '*hijab*' before. What does it mean, anyway?"

I was expecting this question. "In Arabic, the word *hijab* means 'curtain' or 'cover,'" I say after pulling a cue card out from my uniform pocket. "In my religion, Islam, modesty is important for both men and women. Some people think that *hijab* refers to just the head covering Muslim women wear, but actually the word *hijab* also includes the idea of modest dress."

"What's the point of all this covering-up-your-body business?" Stacy remarks in a tone weighed down by self-importance.

"Simple," I respond matter-of-factly. "We believe that building good character and a close relationship with our Creator—*Allah*—is top priority. So in Islam, we value inner beauty over outer appearances, which can be a distraction. One day, all of our earthly beauty will fade, and only the memory of our good deeds and character will remain."

Stacy shakes her head. "Aren't Muslim women *forced* to wear *hijab*?"

"No," I say, crumpling up the cue card in my hand. I decide to speak from my heart. "'Well, it depends. Mostly not. Most Muslim women wear *hijab* as a personal choice."

Juliet chomps down on her bubblegum. "Yeah, right, Farah," she says looking at Tammi for approval.

Juliet gets a favourable nod from her leader, and some other girls also chuckle under their breath.

"Fine, let me put it this way," I declare firmly. "God, Allah, isn't like some big boss in the sky who orders everyone to pray to Him, or to go all day without food or drink during the month of Ramadan, or to give to charity with an open heart. A believer does those things because he or she wants to. In the same way, after a young woman reaches puberty, she has to decide if she'll follow His commandment to cover everything except her hands and face. Some girls start wearing *hijab* when they are very little, because their parents dress them like that so that they can get used to it. Others start when they reach puberty. Some girls find it hard to wear *hijab* when they are teenagers, but they might start when they go to college or get married, or even later when they have children. And some will just start at any time, because they have become more religious. It's like people of any religion; a person might be brought up in a religion, but not necessarily be religious. Or they might end up more religious than their parents; it just depends."

"I don't get it," Stacy remarks, tucking her lead pencil behind her ear. "Don't a lot of feminists think that wearing *hijab* is unfair to women?"

I bite my lip for a moment. "I think that girls and women should work together—not against each other by judging each other's beliefs or styles of dress," I finally say. "Every woman should have the right to choose what she believes is right. If that means wearing *hijab*, then that's her choice. Many Muslims think that *hijabis* are the ultimate feminists because they don't want men or boys to see them as objects. Muslim women want to look respectable in public. At home they can dress up."

"But aren't all those clothes *hot*, Farah?" asks another girl. Several girls nod and murmur.

"Well, the people who live in the hottest parts of the world, like the Sahara desert, wear long, loose clothing. It actually keeps you cooler than wearing tight or short things, because the fabric shades your skin and protects it from the sun's harmful rays, and then when you sweat it cools you down. My Mom says that when you cover up, your skin stays young and healthy. Your hair is also protected from drying out and getting full of dirt and grime. Anyway, that's how most of the people around the world dressed until a few hundred years ago – even in Europe and America."

"Well, if you ask me," Juliet says with an uncontrollable smirk, "*hijabs* are meant for women who have zero fashion sense."

"JULIET!" Ms. Grant exclaims, rising to her full height. "That type of talk is *not* acceptable in this classroom. Do I make myself clear?"

Juliet slumps over her desk like a deflated balloon. "Yes, ma'am."

Ms. Grant smiles at me. "Farah, you've done an excellent job in answering your classmates' questions," she says. "This form of lively debate is exactly what I wanted for this International Women's Day project. Please continue."

She smoothes her knee-length skirt and sits down.

I glance at the familiar faces of the girls in my class and find the courage to go on.

Looking at Juliet, I say, "You're mistaken if you think *hijabs* can't be fashion savvy. Women who wear *hijab* express themselves through fabric choices, patterns and different lengths and styles of *hijab*. There are even *hijab* fashion shows for all-female audiences."

Several of my classmates start to talk at once. My latest statement has started a heated reaction, and I decide to seize the moment.

"Now comes the exciting part of my presentation, ladies!" I reach down to grab a large box that I've kept hidden from view. "As a surprise treat, I've brought in sample *hijabs* for all of you to see. You can pass them around while I demonstrate how they look on real women. I need volunteer models." I raise an eyebrow. "Who wants to be a model?"

Funny enough, Ms. Grant is one of the first volunteers to stick up her hand. Next in line is Ashanti. Then—gasp!—the leader of the 'Cool as Ice' girls, Tammi, says she wants to be a model. Both Ms. Grant and Ashanti quickly file to the front of our classroom.

Tammi sashays towards me, full of confidence. "I know I'll look the best in my *hijab*," she says in a loud stage whisper.

Ms. Grant wags her wise finger at Tammi. "Tsk, tsk, conceit is nobody's friend," she says in an equally loud stage whisper. "Who says these old bones won't look better than you?!"

Everyone in our class laughs at their off-the-cuff theatrics. For the first time ever, Tammi and I smile warmly at each other. Who would have thought that this assignment would help melt the iceberg between us? That thought brings me back to the task at hand.

"Let's get back to business, everyone!" I say, taking charge of my presentation. I pull different *hijabs* from my box. "As I dress up our volunteer models, you can see and touch the different styles of *hijabs* that I'll be passing around. They're all marked with masking tape so you can identify their type."

I hand out *hijabs* in every colour and shape imaginable, and then silently get my models ready, without uttering a word. My hands move expertly as I dress them up. I can hear the oohs and ahhs echoing behind me.

"I just love the fabric on this floral square *hijab*!" I hear someone gush.

"This two-shade *shayla hijab* is cute…" someone else states.

Pretty soon there are more comments circulating than oxygen. I try to contain my excitement, focusing on the job in front of me. Finally, I'm done dressing up my volunteers.

"Eat your heart out, girls! Our models are all set!" I tell my classmates, and their attention quickly moves to the front of the room.

"First we have our glamour girl, Ashanti, who's decked out in a party *hijab*," I say.

Ashanti does a funky twirl so that her look is showcased from every direction. The silver sequins in her *hijab* sparkle under our classroom lights.

"Strike a pose, girlfriend!" I tell Ashanti.

She plants one hand on her cheek and the other on her hip. Ashanti stands frozen on the spot to hold her fashion magazine look.

Our classmates laugh and clap.

"Next we have Tammi," I say. "This Queen of cool has been dressed in a Malaysian crinkle *hijab*."

Tammi does a jaw-dropping spin. The crinkly material of her *hijab* catches her every movement.

"Strike a pose!" I tell her.

Tammi whips her head to the side and arches her back. She, too, freezes like an editorial fashion spread.

My classmates clap with appreciation.

"Last but not least, we have Ms. Grant," I tell everyone. "She's wearing an embroidered under-cap and a flowing Turkish *hijab*."

Ms. Grant gets up and does a sophisticated swirl.

"Ms. Grant's look requires one final touch," I add, while reaching into my box of goodies. I pull out a glittering star-shaped brooch and secure her *hijab* with it, then step back, and turn her face from side to side. "There. You look perfect."

Ms. Grant humbly strikes a pose with the tilt of her chin.

Our teacher gets a standing ovation.

Once everyone settles down, I'm ready to conclude. "Of course, not all Muslim women are interested in fashion, and many prefer plain solid colours, like pastels, white or black. Others wear long *khimar*-style *hijabs* that reach down to the waist. That's just part of the diversity of the Muslim world. I've prepared a handout of different styles of *hijabs* and overgarments worn by women from different countries around the world."

I pass out the handouts while girls lean over them to get a closer look.

"But as for you fashion-conscious types," I continue, "let me reassure you that these colourful scarves will also look ultra-chic wrapped around the neck. And worry not: you don't need to fly across the globe to get hold of these looks..." I pause dramatically, and blow on my henna-decorated fingernails. "As of today, you have a direct connection."

"Really? How?" Stacy asks.

"You're looking at the daughter of a budding businesswoman. My mom doesn't have this huge collection of scarves just for herself: Mom is the co-owner of 'The Hijab Boutique' – our local hotspot for all things Islamic. Think: scarves. Think: inspirational diaries. Think: natural, exotic perfumes. Mention my name, and you'll get a discount." I smile at Stacy. "Come on up, and I'll give you a business card..."

CONCLUSION

It's been one year now since my presentation for International Women's Day at Miss Peabody's. Let's just say a lot has happened. It's about time I got you up to speed!

First of all, Mom and I have moved into a super cute, two-bedroom house with a single garage and a quaint courtyard garden. Our new home may be small, but it's oh-so-cosy, and it's been freshly painted. I keep the weeds out of our front yard and garden because Mom is too busy with the boutique most of the time. My latest project has been designing cards with dried flower petals using the flowers that grow in our garden. I've sold a lot of them, and for each dollar that I earn, I give something to charity and put away some in savings.

Our new neighbourhood is not as chic as our old one, but there's a friendly mosque nearby which has classes and activities for girls my age. It was Mom's idea for me to sign up for the Muslim Girl Scouts. At first I made a face, thinking it would be dorky, but in the end I decided to give it a shot. Boy, am I glad I did! I'm having an amazing time making friends with girls whose mothers are a lot like my mother. It feels great to be able to relate.

As for the 'Cool as Ice' girls, they're still around. Though I don't care so much about what they think anymore. Read: I don't live and breathe for their approval. I guess I'm getting older, and have my own ideas and opinions. I'm happy to report that my social circle has grown. I've got a new friend at the mosque, Amina, who loves art, too. Guess what? We had a fund-raiser for earthquake victims recently, and Amina and I had the idea of putting together shoeboxes to send to women and girls after the last big earthquake. I remembered my Dad's work with the homeless shelters and his idea that "a man's home is his castle", and I figure that a woman's home is her castle, too! So we decorated the frames of unbreakable mirrors that girls and women could hang inside their tents, and included a *hijab* and a small, lightweight prayer carpet in each box – along with a hairbrush, comb, toothbrush, nail file, mini solar flashlight, and a bit of dreamy essential oil perfume, which we hope will make their lives a bit brighter. We included handwritten notes saying, 'Never give up hope – dare to dream!'

You're probably wondering about my 'soul sister,' Ashanti. She and I are still good friends, of course. Sometimes Ashanti models my mother's *hijabs* for her brochures and advertisements, and I take the pictures and do the computer design and layout (I had special classes in graphic design and photography at Miss Peabody's). We have loads of fun doing those brochures!

And The Hijab Boutique? Well, it's going strong. My Mom's looking happy and confident these days, and like she said, *inshallah* we're going to be just fine.